Christmas was coming, and SpongeBob was so excited, he couldn't sleep. He got up to put more decorations on his house.

"There!" he said proudly to Gary. "That's the three-thousandth, one hundredth, and forty-third light. Now let's throw the switch!"

"Beautiful!" cried SpongeBob. "It's even better than last year!"

Next door Squidward leaned out of his window. "SpongeBob!" he yelled sleepily. "How am I supposed to sleep with your lights shining like that?"

"Hi, Squidward!" called SpongeBob. "You're right. My lights need a little something extra. A blanket of fresh snow would be perfect!"

SpongeBob closed his eyes. "I wish for snow on Christmas Day."

Squidward snorted. "I wish for—oh, never mind!"

"Anything's possible with Christmas magic," said SpongeBob. "C'mon. What's your Christmas wish?"

"To have the day off," Squidward grumbled.

SpongeBob shook his head. "But the Krusty Krab is *always* closed on Christmas Day," he said. "You will have the day off."

"Whoopee," said Squidward. "My wish has been granted."

The next morning SpongeBob was all ready to decorate the Krusty Krab. "Mr. Krabs, when should I put up the tinsel?" he asked.

Mr. Krabs frowned. "Hmm . . . let's see. How about half past . . . *never?* Decorations cost too much."

"But Mr. Krabs," sputtered SpongeBob. "It's Christmas! We *have* to decorate the Krusty Krab!"

Mr. Krabs folded his arms. "Give me one good reason, SpongeBob."

Just then someone called out, "Look, everybody! The Chum Bucket has tons of Christmas decorations! And there's a huge line!"

SpongeBob and Mr. Krabs rushed over to the Chum Bucket.

"I heard there's a winter wonderland inside!" a customer said.

"Look at all the lights!" Patrick called out.

Mr. Krabs strode up to Plankton. "Your food's still lousy, Plankton. After the first bite, these customers will run back to the Krusty Krab faster than a flying reindeer!"

But Plankton just laughed. "Ha! Don't you know that at Christmas it's not about the food? It's all about bright lights and fancy trimmings! If you don't decorate, you won't make any money at all!"

Mr. Krabs gulped. "No money?" he said in a small voice.

Mr. Krabs turned to SpongeBob. "Well, what are you waiting for?" he yelled. "Get back to the Krusty Krab and start decorating!"

SpongeBob grabbed Patrick's arm. "C'mon, Patrick, I need your help!"

As they ran back to the Krusty Krab, Plankton watched them go. "This is going to be a very merry Christmas," he said to himself.

SpongeBob and Patrick got to work. "The Krusty Krab is going to be the most festive place in all of Bikini Bottom!" SpongeBob said.

"SpongeBob!" grumbled Squidward. "You're putting up way too many decorations! And what are you doing to that Krabby Patty?"

"Sprinkling it with edible, glow-in-the-dark glitter!" said SpongeBob.

Later Patrick helped with the Reindeer Ride.

"Uuugggh!" he grunted. "It's hard being a reindeer, SpongeBob. I wonder how reindeer do this?"

SpongeBob smiled. "Don't worry, Patrick. It'll be easier once it snows."

"Is it going to snow?" asked Patrick.

"Of course," answered SpongeBob confidently. "That's my Christmas wish. What are you wishing for?"

"A hat made out of chocolate would be nice," said Patrick.

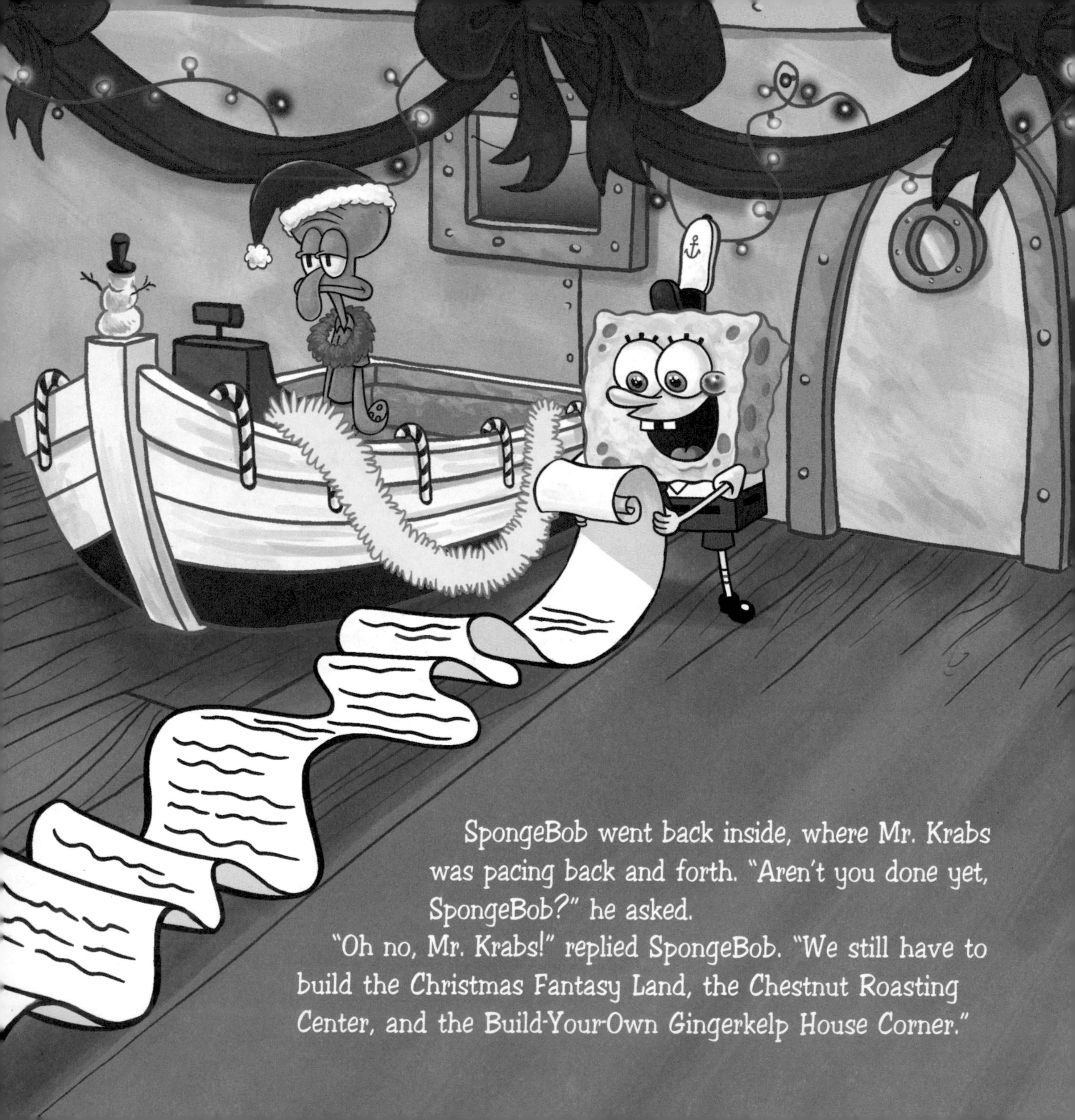

SpongeBob went back inside, where Mr. Krabs was pacing back and forth. "Aren't you done yet, SpongeBob?" he asked.

"Oh no, Mr. Krabs!" replied SpongeBob. "We still have to build the Christmas Fantasy Land, the Chestnut Roasting Center, and the Build-Your-Own Gingerkelp House Corner."

Mr. Krabs frowned. "That sounds like a lot of money."

"But it'll be worth it, Mr. Krabs," SpongeBob insisted. "Everybody will want to come to the Krusty Krab!"

"I hope you're right!" said Mr. Krabs.

The next day it seemed like everyone in Bikini Bottom was at the Krusty Krab! They loved the Christmas decorations and activities—and they bought lots of Krabby Patties.

"SpongeBob, that decorating idea of mine was pure genius! Look at all the customers!" exclaimed Mr. Krabs.

"I know, Mr. Krabs," said SpongeBob. "Everyone's so happy!"

"Well, *I'm* not!" whined Squidward. "I can't wait till Christmas so I can enjoy my day off!"

Mr. Krabs shook his head. "What day off?" he asked. "With this many customers, we're staying open on Christmas Day!"

On Christmas Eve, SpongeBob and Patrick were outside the Krusty Krab, adding even more decorations.

Suddenly Plankton appeared. "Happy holidays, boys! It's too bad Krabs won't let you decorate his restaurant."

SpongeBob was confused. "But, Plankton, we *did* decorate. See?"

Plankton looked at the Krusty Krab. "You call that decorating? I see a bare spot there and there and there . . ."

SpongeBob looked where Plankton was pointing. He was right! There was room for more decorations! SpongeBob quickly added several more strings of lights. Then he flipped the power switch . . .

. . . and the Krusty Krab went dark!

"SpongeBob!" Mr. Krabs yelled.

SpongeBob and Patrick ran into the Krusty Krab. But before SpongeBob could explain, he saw something very strange: a glowing Christmas bow scooting across the floor!

"It's one of my decorated Krabby Patties! It's alive!" SpongeBob said.

Mr. Krabs grabbed a flashlight and shone it on the runaway Krabby Patty—and saw Plankton clinging to the bun! "Why, Plankton, were you trying to steal my secret Krabby Patty recipe *again?*"

"And I would have, if it weren't for SpongeBob's stupid glow-in-the-dark decorations!" Plankton said with a moan.

Just then the sound of jingling bells filled the air.

Everyone rushed outside. It was Santa!

"Ho, ho, ho!" he chuckled. "Looks like someone needs a little Christmas magic!"

Santa reached into a small red bag and pulled out some genuine North Pole snow. He blew it at the Krusty Krab, and all the Christmas lights came back on. And then it started to snow!

"My Christmas wish has come true!" SpongeBob cried.

Santa handed Patrick a present, which he tore open. "Oh, boy!" shouted Patrick. "A hat made out of chocolate! Thanks, Santa!"

That night it snowed so much that the Krusty Krab was closed on Christmas Day. SpongeBob shoveled his way to Squidward's house.

"Merry Christmas, Squidward!" he said. "Your wish came true!"

"You're right, SpongeBob," replied Squidward. "Maybe there's something to this Christmas magic after all."